SAMUEL PEPYS

Dara

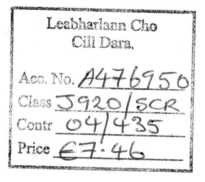
Editors Sarah Ridley, Louisa Sladen
Editor-in-Chief John C. Miles
Design Billin Design Solutions
Art Director Jonathan Hair

First published in 2003
by Franklin Watts
96 Leonard Street
London
EC2A 4XD

Franklin Watts Australia
45-51 Huntley Street
Alexandria
NSW 2015

ISBN 0 7496 4898 8 (hbk)
0 7496 5161 X (pbk)

A CIP catalogue record for this book is available
from the British Library.

Printed in Great Britain

The diary of
SAMUEL PEPYS'S
CLERK

by Philip Wooderson
Illustrated by Brian Duggan

W
FRANKLIN WATTS
LONDON•SYDNEY

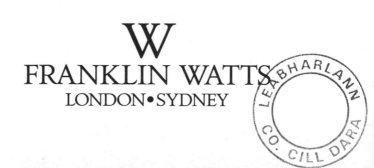

ALL ABOUT SAMUEL PEPYS

This is the diary of Roger Scratch, a fictional sixteen-year-old kinsman (distant relation) of the diarist Samuel Pepys. But who was Samuel Pepys?

Samuel Pepys was born on 23 February 1633 in a room over his father's small tailoring business in Salisbury Court, off Fleet Street, London. He was the fifth of eleven children, eight of whom died in childhood. Although his father had little money he was related to the powerful Montagu family who had a big house and estate near Brampton in Huntingdonshire. One of its leading members, the Earl of Manchester, was a general in Oliver Cromwell's army during the First Civil War (1642-45).

In January 1649 King Charles I was condemned to death and beheaded. As a fifteen-year-old schoolboy, Pepys witnessed the execution at Whitehall. After studying at Cambridge, Pepys was taken on as Edward Montagu's "man of business". Edward Montagu was only a few years older than Pepys but soon became a powerful man in the Navy. Cromwell – by now Lord Protector, head of the republic that was set up following the murder of the King –

promoted him to Joint General of the Navy and Pepys became his secretary.

When Cromwell died in 1659 there was much upheaval between the Army and Parliament. Eventually Edward Montagu was one of the men who invited King Charles II – son of the executed Charles I – back to England from the Netherlands, where he had been living in exile. Pepys was given the task of writing a letter of welcome. Charles rewarded Montagu by making him Earl of Sandwich, and Sandwich rewarded Pepys with an important post on the Navy Board.

It was at this time (1660) that Pepys started keeping his famous diary. He wrote it every day over the next nine years, recording the work he did in reforming the Royal Navy and the great events of the times, including the war with the Dutch, the Great Plague and the Great Fire of London.

Pepys stopped writing his diary because he feared he was going blind; in fact what ailed him was severe eyestrain brought on by too much writing by candlelight! Pepys died at the age of seventy, in 1703.

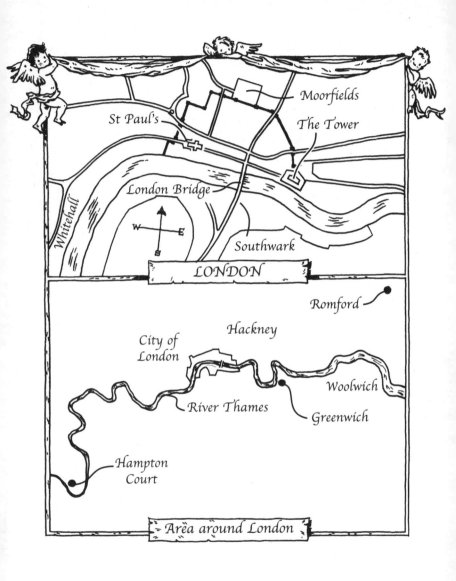

Moorfields

St Paul's

The Tower

Whitehall

London Bridge

W · E
S

Southwark

LONDON

Romford

Hackney

City of
London

Woolwich

River Thames

Greenwich

Hampton
Court

Area around London

I have not got long to live in this dreary dead end town called Brampton. Very soon I shall be on my way. I, Roger Scratch, sixteen years old, have therefore made up my mind to write a diary to keep a record of my Progress in Life.

This will make a fitting memento for my grateful heirs (I hope).

4 MARCH 1665
BRAMPTON, HUNTINGDONSHIRE

Yes, I am going to London. My father has made arrangements for me to take up a post with my (very distant) relative, Mr Samuel Pepys, a gentleman of Great Influence in the King's Navy Office in London. (His mother lives near here – and my school-master put in a word that I was his best pupil – ever.) My mother, who died when I was six, would have been proud of me. My five brothers cannot believe it. After bullying me since birth they now come, cap in hand, asking for me to "remember them", and find them work in the city! They have to be jesting – no chance! They are nothing but unemployed builders (who have to work on our farm). Their greatest ambition in life is to mix up buckets of lime and lug round hods of bricks. I intend to rise by my wits.

These are my ambitions:-

> *To make my fortune before I am twenty-five.*
> *To shine at Court.*
> *I shall want a son and heir, so I will need a wife.*
> *She must be a creature of beauty, though also of*
> *good blood, and must bring me a handsome dowry.*
> *I plan to use some of my fortune to purchase a*
> *country estate. If a man has an income from land*
> *of a thousand pounds per year it is easy to*
> *purchase a peerage (or so says Master Hargreaves,*
> *my school-master in the village).*

At present my savings amount to three pounds four shillings ha-penny. Wish me luck, I have far to go.

5 MARCH 1665

There has been a delay. The cart to take me from Brampton has suffered a broken wheel.

6 MARCH 1665

We finally left at three o'clock this morning. The carter dropped me in Huntingdon, where I caught a public coach for London. I have been in this coach for twelve hours and can hardly hold my quill, I have been so shaken about; but now we have stopped to change horses and I have come into the inn. (The ale is not of good quality. I fear I will have a bad head.)

MUCH LATER
Thank God, I have arrived, though first impressions are not good. We avoided the footpads and robbers who lurk on Stamford Hill, driving at breakneck speed through a small hamlet called Hackney to finally enter the city through Bishop's Gate. But it was too dark to see much.

There were lanterns on some of the main streets, but most of the by-ways were black as pitch, narrow and deep in dung – and not only from four-legged beasts; the residents empty chamber pots out of their upstairs windows, as I found out to my cost. I was splashed after leaving the coach, and when I took my hat off I found it was nesting a turd. What's more, the air is foggy with fumes from so many noxious coal fires.

I had to keep asking the way for Mr Pepys's house. Each time I was directed to look for a different signboard, and with so many lefts and rights I didn't know where I was going.

When I finally found Mr Pepys's house in Seething Lane, I was let in by one of the staff who said, "Ah, the new servant lad!"

I told him, "I'm Mr Pepys's kinsman."

Tom showed me to my "quarters". It seems I must sleep in a cubby-hole, with a curtain for privacy, in the passage just off the kitchen. I thought there had been some mistake, but I tried to make light of the matter.

"At least I am not in the garret," I joked.

Tom told me there isn't a garret because the house has a flat roof (which Mr Pepys likes to use "for holding his summer parties"). The house was once part of a palace which has been divided up to make homes and offices for staff on the Navy Board.

I was invited to sit in the kitchen. This was cosy enough, though much too hot from the fire. The maids are called Alice and Susan. They gave me bread and cheese. Then a sour older woman came in and said she was "Mistress's lady". Her name is Mercer. She told me that Mrs Pepys wished to see me.

I rather like Mrs Pepys, though I am surprised Mr Pepys hasn't told her that I am related. I had to go into great detail about my mother's third cousin being connected by marriage to Mr Pepys's mother's sister. (Or something like that.) But her eyes glazed. She asked for my first thoughts on London. I said it was not much like Brampton. She seemed to find this quite amusing! I think we are going to be friends.

7 MARCH 1665

This morning I woke rather late and felt more optimistic. Venturing out along Cheapside, I saw some fashionable ladies being carried in closed sedan chairs, and even a party of gentry inside a velvet-lined carriage. There were lots of suspicious foreign folk too, speaking strange languages.

I got back to find Mr Pepys sitting down to his dinner. He is older than Mrs Pepys, and plump – with a double chin, but a twinkle in his eye as I sat down to join him, saying how happy I was to be a guest in his house. He said he rather hoped that I would be earning my keep. I said I would be very happy to help on the Navy Board.

"So what are your talents?" he asked me.

I said I could draw a likeness and write rare lines of verse; and anything else that he needed. He said he needed men who could count and write down lists of figures all day without making any mistakes. I said I might find this dull, but everyone has to start somewhere.

Straight after we dined, he took me into his study and wrote down some very hard sums and asked me to give him the answers. I couldn't, not with his fingertips drumming away on the desktop. Then he asked me to copy down a speech he read out – at top speed. It was all about mastheads and topsails. In my haste I knocked over the ink pot.

It was all most humiliating.

8 MARCH 1665

I was sent to deliver some letters today. But most of my time was taken up doing humble tasks set by Mercer. I have polished the pewter and plate and most of the copper pots, just like a common servant!

Tom tells me that war is declared by the Dutch.

10 MARCH 1665

I was taken out shopping with Mistress and had to carry her purchases, including some stinking fish. Not fond of fish myself, but we have it every meal, because it is Lent, I suppose. In fact, Mr Pepys informs me that there is a law in the city banning the eating of meat at this time, not for religious reasons but to help the fishing trade.

11 MARCH 1665

I am doing my best with Mistress, as well as the maids and Tom. But Mercer is not on my side. I think she is telling Master spiteful things about me.

13 MARCH 1665

Master was away on business again so Mistress played the virginals and asked me to sing along: we have an amusing time. Then Master came home late and told her off angrily for putting on new summer clothes. And then I overheard him add: "All because of that coxcomb Scratch!"

Susan says he is over-tired, poor Sir, from all his heavy duties carried out on behalf of our Navy.

19 MARCH 1665

Today Master said he didn't want me left in the house "with the women". He ordered me to follow on foot when he went by coach through Hyde Park. My breeches were covered in dust. However, I glimpsed Lady Castlemaine, one of the beauties at Court! She was older than I expected and fast asleep in her carriage with her mouth wide open.

Now I am exhausted.

20 March 1665

Master went off again; he didn't offer to take me this time. I spent the day with Mistress, escorting her in the afternoon to visit one of her friends. Mrs Flatchett lives in a pleasant house just across the street, so no conveyance was needed. She seemed to be a bit puzzled as to why I had needed to come. I explained that I wasn't a servant, but more of a visiting relative, up to stay from the country.

"Have you seen all the sights?" asked Mrs Flatchett's daughter.

Her daughter is called Henrietta. She is my age. Very pretty. Exactly the sort of young lady I will want as a wife one day. I told her I'm not here for pleasure.

"Mr Pepys is my patron," I said. "I have got great ambitions. I hope to work hard and to prosper."

This seemed to impress Mrs Flatchett. "Will you make a career at the Navy Board?"

"Quite likely, yes," I said boldly, thinking that Mr Pepys could at least get me a post in his own office. Why not? "Though the Board is for older men. I don't want to waste my active years writing out lists of numbers when I could be seeing some action out at sea, on a warship."

Henrietta's mouth dropped open. (Did I say she has lovely blue eyes?)

"Every man must do his duty," I cried, "now we're at war with the Dutch!"

"You mean that you'll go out and fight?" she asked, in an admiring tone.

"If needs be, of course!"

This evening, music with Mistress: Mr Pepys was home again late, and found us drinking sweet wine. But rather than getting angry he gave us a hazy smile and disappeared into his study. Mistress was strangely flustered. Sending me after him, she wanted me to give him his night cap to protect his head from the cold "and find out what he's been getting up to". I found him at his desk.

I spoke but he failed to hear me. Leaning over his shoulder I thought he was making an entry in a small, leather-bound volume, then realised he was actually writing on a small scrap of paper on top of the book. I read this much: "My dearest, sweetest Molly, what fun we–"

Then he swung round. "Mister Scratch!"

He brushed the note to one side, and held out the volume. "See this? Do you think you have found me out – as a Catholic spy?"

"No," I stuttered, thinking he's drunk.

"But I might be writing down valuable information from the Navy Office to send to the King of France! You really are far too trusting."

I told him calmly but firmly that I knew him to be a man of great honour.

"So what do you think I am up to?"

"Perhaps, Sir," I ventured a guess, playing along with his ruse, ignoring his letter to "Molly" – "like me you are keeping a diary?"

He stared at me in surprise. "Well done, Mr Scratch – how astute!"

"But why do you write it in code?" I asked.

"Not code but shorthand, Scratch; a method for writing more quickly, often used by the ladies in church, when they want to take notes from the sermon. You'd be well-advised to learn it yourself. But what do you put in your diary?"

I said that I'm keeping a record, "For my descendants to read, Sir – that they might discover how I made my way in the world."

He looked intrigued. "Very good; but how do you plan to do that?"

I said I will work for my living, given the chance. (Hint, hint.)

He nods. "The harder you work, Scratch, the further you'll get."

"I'd work hard, Sir, if you could just find me a post?"

He frowned. He pulled a slight shrug. "Very well then, we'll strike a bargain." He put on the padded night-cap then held out his hand to me.

"You promise to not say a word about my "celebrations", either in your diary, or to my wife. And also, if you would be so good as to deliver this letter–" he turned and stuffed it into an envelope, "tonight, to Molly Goodall, at the Angel Tavern." He pressed it into my hand. "In exchange I will do my best to make a good clerk of you, Scratch!"

22 MARCH 1665

I have to say that Master showed confidence in me today. He had the kindness to take me with him to an important social engagement at the house of Sir William Petty, the man who Master replaced as Treasurer on the Committee. The Duke of Albemarle was there, a big ungainly man, with Lord Sandwich – who is Master's great patron; both of them high in the Navy. Also, some gorgeous ladies including Mrs Middleton, a favourite at the King's Court! I was totally awe-struck.

Sir William talked at great length about the terms of his will. He wanted to leave a fair sum to reward men for great inventions.

"What sort of inventions?" asked Master. Sir William suggested that he would be most glad to have scientific knowledge of how women made the milk to come in their breasts. I thought this so disgusting I could not hide my reaction so he asked ME what invention I thought would deserve a reward.

"Surely, Sir," I suggested, doing my best to sound thoughtful, "it ought to go to whoever can rise to the challenge of turning base metal to gold?"

"Whoever does that will hardly need MY reward," said Sir William.

Everyone found this so funny, including the beautiful ladies, my face burnt red with the shame. I did not dare open my mouth again for the rest of the evening. I was glad when we left at last.

26 MARCH 1665
EASTER SUNDAY

I have written nothing these last few days because I have been so down about being publicly embarrassed.

To make matters worse, I was out in the lane on Good Friday morning when Henrietta went by, with her mother and father, all on their way to church.

"Still here?" said Mr Flatchett, a short and sharp, edgy man. "I gathered from my daughter you had volunteered for the Navy!"

Henrietta was looking so lovely I said I would soon be gone. "I have only a few days left, Sir."

Henrietta looked close to tears. But afterwards I felt extra sore that I have no formal position. In fact I'm no more than a servant without any proper duties other than doing my best to keep Mistress in good cheer, which is not always easy.

(So much for my training in clerkdom!)

She keeps asking what I know about Master's late night meetings. In the end I had to confess he might be out "celebrating" at the Angel Tavern.

On Saturday night Master came home late, yes, even later than usual, from meeting "a friend" as he puts it, and matters came to a head.

Many cross words were spoken, with Mistress calling on me to agree what a sad, lonely life she now has.

"Not with Scratch at your beck and call," Master said, and Mistress stormed out in a huff. I asked Master what he meant by this, but he knew he had gone too far. He told me to mind my own business.

But then this morning he greeted me as sweet as ever could be, wishing me happy Easter. And when I returned the greeting, he told me with a wide smile that this is his own special day, "The day when I always celebrate," (oh no!) "getting rid of a vile intruder!" I thought he meant me for a moment but he said, "No, don't worry, young Scratch. This was an inanimate object, which I will show you later."

After a splendid dinner of roast meats and curd tarts, with rather a lot of fine wines, Master took me aside and brought something out of a wooden box kept on his desk in his study. With this behind his back he gave me a solemn lecture. He said that when he was only my age he had neither money nor prospects.

"And London was not the place it is now. Half the shops had closed, trade was ruined because of the Civil War; and what's more I wished to marry."

He raised his eyebrows at me. "Of course I was fortunate, Scratch. I had Edward Montagu, who is now Lord Sandwich, as a distant relation. He took me on as his man of business. But this would have done me no good if I had died from the pain in my bladder!"

I cannot believe what I'm hearing.

"Yes, Scratch, the pain; it got so bad that my only hope was the surgeon. I said my prayers and they tied me down on the kitchen table, then the doctor set to work with his knife. I almost passed out from the agony, but well within the minute he whipped this out of me."

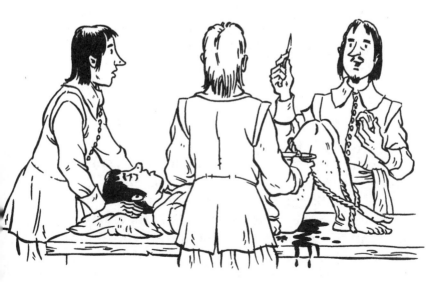

Master held up a stone the size of a tennis ball. "It had been blocking my bladder. A bladder stone, Scratch. From that moment I felt like a man re-born – and I was determined to work all hours to make a success of my life."

"As you have, Sir," I had to admit. "And what's more, I'll treasure your example and make a success of MY life. Have you thought about training me yet, Sir?"

His eyebrows rose and fell. I might as well fight for my country!

17 APRIL 1665

I haven't joined up so far, and today we heard the news of a fierce battle at sea. Three Dutch ships have been captured; the brave captain of the *Diamond* killed in the fight.

I told Tom of my plan to enlist. He said it's the surest way to get my head blown off – or make a pile of money. Well, that's more like it! "How so?" I asked.

"From prizes," he said. "If one of our ships captures an enemy vessel, the goods all get shared out. Some of it goes to the King but the crew still get their cut – and if it's a merchant ship full of treasures from the Indies you stand to make serious money!"

23 APRIL 1665

Attended a service at Whitehall Chapel this Sunday, thanks to Master and Mistress, and heard "the famous Stillingfleet"; Edward Stillingfleet, who Master knew at Cambridge. He has recently been appointed as one of the King's chaplains, on account of his brilliant sermons. Not that I followed the sermon. I was thinking about my own future.

To be useful to Master (a Man of Great Influence), I must learn what I can about his naval business. The other day he helped me in this when he took me to Tower Hill, on a tour round all the warehouses that supply the needs of the fleet. We have 16,000 seamen, all requiring daily rations. To supply each one with his rations the going rate is six pence per day in peacetime, and eight pence now we're at war, but Master says that the system is failing. The money is not enough, and much of it disappears into the pockets of corrupt officials: the food is often so rancid that ships cannot stay at sea without their sailors starving or catching disgusting diseases. (Just as well I didn't enlist.)

Master wants to reform the system, to make it more efficient to help us beat the Dutch, but he fears it is now too late. The enemy is ready to put to sea any day. Our dockyards lack masts and ropes, the Navy has massive debts and we don't even have enough seamen. Only press-gangs can bring new recruits; these are gangs that go out and compel men to enlist in the Navy. They have even been rounding up schoolboys!

I have to put it to Master that with the Navy in debt, how can the war be paid for? He says Parliament has voted to raise a new tax, but this will take time to collect, and meanwhile the richest men in the land are lending money to the King – at a high rate of interest. "Is that what you do?" I asked him, intrigued.

He spluttered that he is not rich, only comfortably off.

28 APRIL 1665

Thanks to my paying attention over these last few days, Master took me with him when he went to inspect some warships moored on the river, downstream. It was fine to set out on the Navy Board's yacht, to see all the river traffic and look back on our great city, with the great roof of St Pauls looming over the chimney tops.

But what Master saw of the ships put him in a foul mood. None of them had been loaded up with the provisions they needed, so they were in no fit state to sail against the Dutch.

At least we were back for dinner, but afterwards Master stormed off and shut himself in his study in order to write a long letter, describing what he had seen. This put Mistress in a bad mood. She said she would need me to cheer her up. And thus I missed my chance to go to Whitehall with Master when he went to deliver his letter to the Council Chamber.

Instead, getting out my brushes, I gave Mistress a painting lesson. She found this all very intriguing. And in exchange she offered to give me a dancing lesson. She got Mercer to play on the virginals while she showed me the steps, but somehow my heart wasn't in it.

When Master came home he told us that he had been well-received by the Duke of Albemarle – who had read the letter at once and shown it to His Majesty, King Charles the Second himself.

"Was His Majesty cross," I asked, "about the state of His ships?"

"Very concerned," agreed Master. "Yet pleased by my diligence, too."

So Master was in a good mood. We all settled down, quite happy, sharing a very good supper; though later on Master mentioned an outbreak of plague in the city. But I dare say that this will blow over, as it did back in Brampton last year.

29 APRIL 1665

Master told me his mother is coming to stay; the lady who first proposed that I should be sent up to London. As she is coming from Brampton she will bring news of home, from my father! I'm surprised how excited this makes me. Master says I can teach HER to paint too: "… and you can dance with her if you like, Scratch!"

I am not sure if he was joking.

1 MAY 1665
A MEMORABLE DAY

I was out and about with Master when a most impressive carriage drew up. Master was hailed by the occupants who seemed to know him well and insisted he climb on board. (I only just managed to leap on the back as the carriage shot off down the street.)

A boat was waiting at Tower Wharf. From here we were rowed down river, all the way to Greenwich where another coach was waiting. This one was rather smaller and I had to run behind it, nearly choking to death on the dust.

The gentlemen took dinner with someone called Colonel Blunt (though I was fed in the kitchen, just like a common servant). Afterwards the Colonel showed us around his vineyard. Master said he had never seen such a thing.

"Imagine, being able to make your own wine!" he said, and everyone nodded sagely.

Next, the Colonel took us into a barn to show us his prize exhibits – various wicker baskets supported on lots of springs. He said he would be much obliged if we would take it in turns to sit ourselves down in these baskets, to test the level of comfort while they were rocked about. Master told me to do the rocking. Thus I never got a go, and I couldn't see the point, until the Colonel explained that his aim was to find a way of making a coach run more smoothly than on the usual supporting straps.

His favourite was a gigantic spring so strong it could take the weight of a whole carriage all by itself. But with only one man in a basket sitting on top it bounced wildly; so much that one of its occupants, a certain Mr Hooke, had to rush outside. I think he puked into the bushes.

Afterwards, back in the carriage (suspended on ordinary straps) we carried on to Deptford to visit Mr Evelyn, another of Master's friends.

He seems to know lots of people like these, all learned and scientific. They are members of something called The Royal Society. This was set up to investigate "the paradoxes of nature".

It was late by the time we arrived at Mr Evelyn's house, and too dark for us to inspect Mr Evelyn's beautiful garden. Master made an arrangement to come back another day. On the way home, by ourselves, I had a word with Master about how he was treating me. He made a very strange comment – that a dog that stood on its hind legs would still be a dog. Very odd.

5 MAY 1665

Master's mother arrived and closeted herself upstairs. She has brought a letter from home! I opened it in my cubby-hole, but it is a bit of a let-down. Hardly any news, except of a sow having piglets, and my brothers wanting to know what success I have had in finding them building work here! Let them go hang, that's what I say.

24 MAY 1665

Another gap in my diary, but what can I write about? My hopes of fame and fortune have not found much success, considering I've now been in London for more than two full months! I partly blame the Dutch: war is all that anyone talks about (apart from their fears of the plague, which seems to be getting worse), and Master has no time to carry on with my "training". At least, that's how he puts it. He says that a hundred warships and countless fire-ships have set sail from Holland against us. Perhaps I should volunteer for the Navy? Right now I am only wasting my life looking after Master's mother. She looks just like him, only fiercer, and wants to play at cards all the time.

28 MAY 1665

What blessed relief! Master took me on a visit to Lady Sandwich. She is the wife of Master's great patron, who is at sea with the fleet, and lives in a splendid house. We talked about one of their captains, who is condemned to be shot for "failing to engage his ship in battle". In other words, being a coward!

Lady Sandwich is, however, more concerned about a Scandal at Court. Apparently Lord Rochester has tried to run away with a beautiful widow and heiress known as Mrs Mallett. The lady was on her way home, having supped at Whitehall with the King, when her carriage was stopped at Charing Cross – by Lord Rochester's men! The lady has still not been found but the King is so angry about it that His Lordship is shut in the Tower!

It seems that Lady Sandwich has had her eye

on the lady as a possible wife for her son. This
would be nice for him because Mrs Mallett will
be worth two-and-a-half thousand pounds a year
– as soon as her mother is dead.

Is marriage my best course of action? I'd have to
find a young heiress, of course – not so easy
without a title. Lady Sandwich's son has more spots
than me but he's called Lord Hinchingbrooke!
I wish I was called Lord Scratch. Then I could
have Mrs Mallett, though I would prefer
Henrietta. I wonder what her father's worth?

Whatever, my chances are slim, unless I can
SHINE in some way. If only I could invent
something special and claim some kind of
reward from the Royal Society... I must give this
matter more thought.

30 MAY 1665

I have given the matter more thought. I don't
think I'll get very far unless I can find a real
patron. (Master is totally useless.) First, I must
have an idea though, something to make an
impression. I need to draw up some plans.

1 JUNE 1665

After dinner Master got dressed in a most
imposing new suit which Mistress lets it be known
has cost him one guinea, four shillings. (This is
more than I earn in a month as Master's humble
servant, for that's all I am, at this juncture!) Then

he and Mistress went off to the funeral of Sir Thomas Viner, who was the Mayor of London about ten years ago. This left me free until supper!

I set off through the city in pursuit of my mission. On my way I noticed crosses marked on several doors. I know what they portend – houses visited by the plague! I gave them all a wide berth. This made for a much longer walk, but finally I was over London Bridge and out in open fields. I made my way to Greenwich. When I reached the Colonel's house I found him out in his barn tinkering with his "suspensions". I told him what I am about. He said he'll happily take me on, as his "part-time assistant". This wasn't quite what I meant but... a step in the right direction!

3 JUNE 1665

The battle begins! From the rooftop we hear the guns, echoing up the river. Our fate is being decided. Master is concerned about his patron, Lord Sandwich, who is commanding the fleet.

6 JUNE 1665

Three days of rumours: is it victory or defeat? No certain news from the Fleet.

Master took me to visit Lady Sandwich. She is in a wild state, though less in fear for her husband than over the Scandal at Court.

Lord Rochester is disgraced, so now her hopes are high yet again for her son to marry the heiress!

7 JUNE 1665

Too hot to write: it is sweltering outside, and I'm sweating away like a pig. I am in terror that this is a symptom that I've caught the plague. Just my luck.

8 JUNE 1665

Momentous news: I am feeling completely better. Also, Master tells us of a Great Victory, off the coast at Lowestoft. The Dutch are completely routed. Flags have been hung from the windows of Henrietta's house. I am now having second thoughts about not volunteering for the Navy. Perhaps I could do so today and claim that I signed up last week?

17 JUNE 1665

I have learnt more about the great battle from some of the leading men as they have returned to Court, all ruddy-faced from being at sea and flushed with gallantry!

It seems Lord Sandwich did bravely, but nobody speaks of him. This is to play up the derring-do of the Right Royal Duke of York who, it seems, was knocked off his feet after the man standing next to him had his head taken off by a cannonball. The head hit him in the stomach and sent him flying – head over heels, ha-ha!

There is also more bad news about the spread of the plague. As Master was coming home today in a hackney coach, the driver was suddenly taken ill. Master was forced to get off and find another carriage. Master says 112 people have died of the plague within the last week. The gentry are fleeing the city. Master's mother has gone back to Brampton, taking a letter from me to my folks, telling them how in this time of plague they can forget about building work!

There are plans for Mistress to leave too. She wants me to go with her, because I "encourage her so" in her new interest of painting. This would be safer for me, but Master makes the decision. Strangely he tells her he needs me; so she'll have to make do with Mercer. This means I can get on with the Project and take my chances!

20 JUNE 1665

Something more cheerful! Today was a Thanks-giving Day for our victory over the Dutch. Master went celebrating at the Dolphin Tavern, leaving the servants free in the kitchen to heartily eat and drink, and later there were bonfires, with fiddlers and dancing too.

Not that I wanted to dance. On the way home I paused to look up at Henrietta's lighted window – and she looked down on me. For a moment I know that our eyes met.

23 JUNE 1665

Tonight Master came home late, his clothing much dishevelled but in a mighty good humour. Today, at a meeting, Lord Sandwich turned up unexpectedly. The Admiral told them how the King's cousin had not been so brave in the battle as we had been led to believe!

"At the start of the fight Prince Rupert's ship was in the front line by mistake, but after that", Master chuckled, "it seems he did his utmost to sail it clean out of danger!" Then Master turned serious and warned me against idle gossip: "Prince Rupert's a fine enough chap, Scratch."

As for Lord Sandwich, his close brush with death has set him worrying about his children's futures, says Master.

"His Lordship must go back to sea to chase the Dutch again, so he has left it with me to arrange for his daughter to marry the son of Sir George Carteret. You know who HE is, do you, Scratch?"

"The Treasurer of the Navy, Sir?"

"Well done, Scratch; you are learning fast."

25 JUNE 1665

Master has made approaches to Sir George Carteret and says he has won his approval, which doesn't seem so surprising, for even though Sir George's son hasn't set eyes on the girl yet Lord Sandwich intends his daughter to have £5,000 outright, plus £800 a year. I'd marry a horse for that much money!

30 JUNE 1665

Three hundred have died of the plague this week, within the city walls, and the Court is leaving Whitehall. I don't like this one little bit!

9 JULY 1665

Master spends every evening out, "doing his gallivanting" as Mercer would have put it. Tonight, coming home, loose-tongued with drink, he told me: "What you should do, Scratch, is go out and pick up some wenches."

I told him that's all very well, but living the high life costs money which, sadly, I don't have (as yet).

He said, "Hummm, all in good time, Scratch."

But the plague might take me tomorrow! Master seems to enjoy this plague time – perhaps he likes dicing with death? But then, it's all right being his age, with all his achievements behind him. If I die, it's more of a waste.

10 July 1665

Master told me about this wedding plan. He has met Sir George's son, young Philip Carteret. "A modest fellow," he told me. "Most pleasant and interesting in his own way; he took part in the fight with the Dutch. But he's so damnably shy I can't think how he'll manage to win round a pretty young lady!"

13 July 1665

Worse news concerning the plague – more than 700 dead within the last seven days: where will they put all the corpses? The churchyards are stinking already.

Yesterday was proclaimed "a day of solemn fasting" but none of us took any notice. I don't see how it would help. "Eat and drink while you can," as Tom says.

This is Master's philosophy, too.

14 July 1665

We went by water to Deptford, where the Carterets have a fine house. It was wonderfully cool on the river, with a fresh breeze blowing away all the stinking vapours of London. We found Lady Sandwich there. She was keen to show Master her purchases of glass, fine bedding and plate for the wedding. Her daughter, Lady Jemima, has gone up to "Dagenhams", their country estate near Romford in Essex. Master has been invited to visit there at the weekend, and the Carterets will come too. Sir George wants Master to tell his son "about the birds and the bees".

15 July 1665

We all met up again, at Greenwich in the morning, where Colonel Blunt came to greet us. He is lending the party his carriage (with normal, standard suspension). We crossed the river by ferry, the guests going first, with the horses, leaving me to follow behind with the coachman and carriage. This gave me time to look underneath, to see how it is suspended on leather straps from the axles. My method should be an improvement, but only if the Colonel's men do the work as I suggest it. By the time we had crossed the river I'd drawn some useful diagrams and hidden them inside my vest. Eventually, after a tiring drive, we reached "Dagenhams".

The mansion is very imposing and there are dozens of servants, most too high and mighty to speak to me.

Later Master told me that Sir George had proposed that the couple ought to be left alone "so they can start their *amours*". But Master, as the great expert, had cautioned against this course, in case the young man was too sudden and gave the young lady a scare!

"More likely the other way round!" I said.

"Oh, he likes the young lady," said Master. "At least he claims that he does, though not so much that she'd notice, or think he'd take the trouble to try to make her his wife."

"So what will happen tomorrow?" I asked.

Master looked at me shrewdly. "They'll meet up at church, I expect. But before that…" He gave me his slow, greasy grin – the one he always uses when he is calculating, "… Sir George is going to send the young man so I can give him some coaching."

"Coaching?" I said. "In what way, Sir?"

Then Master took hold of my arm.

"I'd be very grateful to you, Scratch, if you could be there, in the gallery, just to give me some help, nothing arduous. I'll tell you more when the time comes."

16 JULY 1665
SUNDAY

We rendezvoused in the gallery. This was a long, panelled hall stretching the length of the house on the first floor, lined with paintings. I got to know some of them well, having to wait for Master who turned up very late.

Mister Philip turned up later than Master. Then up and down all three of us paced; me keeping a step behind Master as he instructed young Carteret on how to approach a lady with "gentle grace and decorum".

"There naturally comes the moment to gently take hold of her hand, and that is best accomplished with a slight compliment, on how well the lady is looking. Now try it," said Master, beckoning to me from behind. "Just use your imagination. Pretend that young Scratch is Jemima."

(A page has been torn out here.)

After some thought I've decided to spare my descendants and heirs from having to share the embarrassment that Mr Pepys put me through. It was very unpleasant. Mister Philip might be a bit feeble, but he's still got a bristly chin.

17 July 1665

We left "Dagenhams". Master gave large tips to the servants. (I shall tell Tom about this.) Later Master informed me that he managed to "steal a moment" to have words with Lady Jemima, to ask how she liked Mister Philip. "She hid her face in her hands and said she'd obey her father, to do what he thinks is best!"

This seemed to satisfy Master as "being the best we can hope for".

And what about her, I thought?

20 JULY 1665

The Bills of Mortality show 1,089 people dead of the plague last week. Thank God, so far I've been spared. Master says that Lady Carteret has given him a bottle of "strange and powerful water that is a sure cure for the plague" – as a reward, I suppose, for helping "arrange" this marriage.

25 JULY 1665

The town is near empty and quiet, and Master away for the day, gone to Hampton Court attending on the King. In the meantime I have been busy supervising our local blacksmith to make two pairs of fine springs. (I'm hoping Colonel Blunt will settle the bill for this.)

26 JULY 1665

A memorable day, for Master took me out of town to Greenwich – to meet His Majesty King Charles the Second, who came from Hampton

Court to visit some building works there.

They all spoke some while with Master and, when it was time to leave, the King invited Master to travel with them on their barge. I was allowed along too, as an "Honorary Footman".

At Woolwich we disembarked and Master found some time to pay a quick visit on Mistress. She showed him her latest paintings. Master told me afterwards he found them "exceeding curious".

27 JULY 1665

Master was summoned to Hampton Court to bid farewell to the King before Their Majesties set off on their journey to Salisbury. Thus I had more time in the blacksmith's smoky forge. The two pairs of springs are completed. The bill is far more than I'd feared.

28 JULY 1665

The weekly bill reports another 1,700 dead of the plague in London. Today we had to make another long journey to "Dagenhams". We found the household much afraid, as the chaplain who gave the sermon last week died of plague two days ago. Nobody knows how he caught it! But everyone is in agreement that the marriage should not be delayed for fear that death might take off one of the (un)happy pair – so plans are afoot for Monday. I hope this will leave me time to sort out the Colonel's carriage!

30 July 1665

My day off: I have spent it in Colonel Blunt's barn. After six hours very hard labour we have the carriage set up; its leather straps replaced with iron bars and chains linked to my two pairs of springs, exactly as I had intended.

I mentioned the cost to the Colonel. He said he would "wait and see if it works". Then claim the credit, no doubt! I wonder if I have been wise to put my trust in this man? I have to look on the bright side. If all goes according to plan, we shall drive to "Dagenhams" in such rare comfort and style that we will get there ahead of our schedule, and all the guests at the wedding will want their carriages "sprung" according to the Scratch Method. And I will be well on my way not only to fame and fortune, but also to the more precious project of wooing my Heart's Desire!

31 July 1665
The Wedding Day of Lady Jemima and Mister Philip Carteret

It was agreed that I should collect the Colonel's carriage in time to be at Deptford for six o'clock, Monday morning, ready to cross on the ferry and meet the parents with Master on the north bank of the river.

Alas, my new pairs of springs proved inadequate to take the weight of the carriage. Before we had got to the ferry they had been stretched out so long that the bottom of the carriage was bumping upon the cobbles. We had to turn back. Then a chain snapped, dislocating one axle. By the time the coachman had run all the way back to the barn for the straps, and come back with enough helpers to fit the wheel back on the carriage, the ferry had missed the tide, so we had to wait three more hours. And all the time we were waiting I was aware of Master on the opposite shore, pacing up and down in the blustery breeze.

I expected him to be furious, to beat me with his cane. But when at last the carriage was rolled off the ferry boat, Master was patience itself. He said that the marriage licence and the wedding ring had been despatched by horseman, so the ceremony at "Dagenhams" could proceed if we were late. Of course, we were very late. We got there to find the house empty, and only reached the church as the congregation filed out.

The bridegroom was in his ordinary clothes

because he "had lacked the confidence to put on his own wedding finery" without Master there to assist! So Lady Jemima had followed his lead and she hadn't dressed up either.

The wedding feast was no better. Hardly a goblet was emptied, and supper was even more gloomy, their talk all about the plague; followed by evening prayers, then everyone off to bed. But Master insisted I come with him to the bridegroom's chamber, bringing a bottle of Malaga wine to keep the young man relaxed. By the time Mister Philip was summoned to go to his young bride's chamber he needed help to stand up. But Master had the privilege of seeing them both to bed and kissing the bride good night before drawing the curtains on them and tiptoeing out of the room.

I took this moment to tell him that I was deeply sorry for having delayed the carriage and spoilt the wedding day.

But Master took my arm, and leading me back down the passage, told me that, all in all, things had turned out as well as they could. "You were just trying to make your mark, or make your scratch, eh Scratch? There's nothing like an experiment for learning the facts of a matter… though possibly the Colonel could have had the good sense to make you wait a few days. Though these are such times, I grant you, such times as man must make haste. Two thousand dead of the plague in a week! We might both be gone Monday next; so God preserve us as friends in good health!" His voice was slurred by the wine. Then he gave me a fatherly hug. "Let no more be said about springs."

Fair enough; except they still have to be paid for!

15 AUGUST 1665

I have not written my diary in these last two weeks, feeling so glum about life, the business about the springs robbing me of my hopes (and nearly all my savings). Henrietta and her family have quit Seething Lane leaving their house shuttered up, and I daresay they will not return until this plague is finished.

More than three thousand dead in the last seven days! The Mayor has passed an order to shut up the sick in their homes to stop them infecting the healthy, only allowing them out for air after nine at night, when the healthy must stay indoors.

Tonight, Master turned up white as a sheet, having come face to face with a victim down on the churchyard steps. "His neck was swollen, his eyes were wild, the image of death," Master told me.

He has also heard from Salisbury that one of the grooms with the King has gone down sick with plague, so the Court will be packing their bags to move from Salisbury to Milton.

Now most of the shops are shut up, the churchyards are overflowing, the air is reeking of death, and as I write these words I hear more carts going by, laden with putrid corpses. Pits have been dug in the fields, outside the city walls,

and bodies are dumped without ceremony, just coated with lime to dissolve them. I pray that I should be spared this fate. I sit in my cubby-hole under the stairs burning herbs to cleanse the air of any invading vapours – and practically cough to death.

I never have felt so anxious, yet strangely, Master stays cheerful.

27 AUGUST 1665

Master has been kept busy at his office or down at Sheerness, then Windsor, then Greenwich again, seeing to matters of business. The fleet has been forced to return to port in order to get more provisions, though now, as our ships head back to sea, to take on the Dutch again, Master has made up his mind at last that we should pack up house and leave for the fresh airs of Woolwich!

31 AUGUST 1665

The Bills of Mortality for this week show six thousand poor souls dead of the plague. Master reckons this optimistic. "More likely TEN thousand!" he said.

"Will any of us be spared?" I asked.

He chuckled at me, "Cheer up, Scratch! We're both a great deal healthier than we've any right to expect. Enjoy life, that's my prescription!"

With that, he went out for the night.

3 SEPTEMBER 1665

Still cheerful, Master appeared this morning wearing his fine coloured suit and holding a new periwig. He told me with a glint in his eye that he had not worn this before. "I bought it after the plague broke out; it's guaranteed pure human hair – probably clipped from the head of a plague victim's corpse!"

And off he went, with his new wig on his head, leaving me with Tom to carry on packing up house as fast as we possibly can. We're frantic to leave the city – though as I say to Tom, "It's no good getting away if we go with Master and he's caught the plague – he'll infect us!" But Tom thinks Mr Pepys would have got it by now and have died if he was going to get it.

5 SEPTEMBER 1665

Today I was highly embarrassed, as well as cross and resentful, when Colonel Blunt turned up. I tried to ask about money but he brushed this aside with a laugh, insisting we come outside to take a look under his carriage. It was balanced upon a single, gigantic iron spring. He claimed it a total success. "Enables the horses to tear along at twice their normal speed and gives a man double the comfort! You need to be bold to succeed, Scratch. Your scheme was too complicated, what with those chains and those piddly springs – the Blunt System's far more MANLY!"

7 September 1665

Yesterday's Bill of Mortality showed 7,000 dead in a week! Master said we should leave straightaway.

The streets were foggy with smoke from bonfires on every junction, lit to chase away the foetid vapours of plague. I saw so many crosses on doors, and coffins taken on carts even though this was during the day time and strictly against the Mayor's orders. I saw corpses afloat on the river.

Reached Woolwich and Mrs Pepys greeted me most warmly.

10 September 1665

Mistress tells me her father is now taken ill of the plague, and as she has been with him I wonder if she is contagious?

16 September 1665

Over the last few days I have been left with Mistress, trying to cheer her up after the death of her father, while Master goes off on business. He came home haggard one night, no longer full of good cheer but only dire tales of the plague; all the people he's known who have died, along with their poor young children. Mistress calls this a blessing; far kinder than leaving them orphans.

17 SEPTEMBER 1665

Went out with Master, on the yacht from the
Navy Board, to check on the state of our fleet, as
there is news that Lord Sandwich has broken off
from fighting the Dutch and our ships are now
in the estuary. We sailed down river to
Gravesend where we moored for the night.

18 SEPTEMBER 1665

It was a splendid sight; a hundred vessels at
anchor, with our three principal ships bedecked
in many flags. Master was welcomed on board
the nearest ship, the *Prince*, and Lord Sandwich
came out to greet us, wearing only his night
gown. Master wanted to know why has he not
kept the fleet at sea, to carry on pounding the
Dutch? His Lordship blamed lack of provisions
and the plague. Master shook his head grimly.

However, this sorry state of affairs is not as

bleak as it might be. Our fleet has managed to capture a convoy of Dutch merchant ships. These are loaded with valuable cargoes of silks and spices from the Indies. These prize goods should please the King!

20 SEPTEMBER 1665

On our way back on the yacht I asked Master what the King would do with all those Dutch goods? Master said that the King's Commissioners would naturally want to take them, in order that they might sell them to raise what money they could. Then some of the money would be returned so as to be divided between the officers and their crews. "It's a long ponderous process," he said.

As we sailed back up river I carried on thinking this over. In desperate times, I reckoned, desperate measures were needed. Master was all for efficiency. Why not with this matter of prizes? I was starting to get some ideas. I wondered if this was my chance to make a mark at last?

22 SEPTEMBER 1665

Today Master took me with him, along with a Captain Cocke, to visit the new dock at Blackwall. Lord Sandwich was there. While they talked I started thinking again, and later I put it to Master that I had thought of a chance to do some useful business, to benefit everybody.

"I don't quite follow you, Scratch."

I reminded him of what he had said, quite a long time ago, about taxes raised by Parliament taking too long to collect. "And in the meantime, you told me, rich gentlemen lend the money, to tide the King over."

"Yes, Scratch?"

"Well, what if the same happens here, I mean with the prize goods?"

"How so?"

"Sir, if the prize goods were sold off right away, instead of being taken ashore and locked in a warehouse for weeks, waiting for the Commissioners to get round to dealing with them, everybody might benefit – including yourself – if you bought them."

Master frowned into the distance.

"I don't see why I would want to, unless I could sell them again?"

"Exactly, Sir; sell at a profit!"

He gave me his greasy grin. "A pity I've not got the money, Scratch, so the whole thing is out of the question."

"Not in the least!" This was Captain Cocke. "It sounds like a good plan. Remember, Pepys, I was saying last night we should make an investment: we'd get the goods at a discount; I'd soon sell them on at a profit! Mind you, there's no time to be wasted. From what I've heard, some officers have been helping themselves already. Be bold, Pepys: talk to Lord Sandwich!"

23 SEPTEMBER 1665

I am in high esteem: the captain clearly considers me a man of great vision in business, and even Master himself has shown me some sly regard. If this goes well he will owe me a post in the Navy Office – and a percentage, of course! (The Flatchetts will look at me then!)

25 SEPTEMBER 1665

Back to the fleet. We boarded the *Prince* again, and Master spent a long while in conference with Lord Sandwich – offering him £5,000 for silk, cinnamon, nutmegs and indigo. He seemed very bold to begin with, though later it seemed to me that the deal might have come unstuck had Captain Cocke not stepped in. A bargain was finally struck with Captain Cocke as his partner, taking half the purchase.

Afterwards I wondered where so much money would come from? I ventured to ask.

"Don't presume, Scratch!" Master glowered at me – as if it was none of my business!

Later, a junior officer said it is common knowledge that, "Mr Pepys will take out a loan from the Admiral's own deputy treasurer, out of the naval funds that are needed to pay the poor seamen!"

I suppose this means he must be sure he can

sell on the goods straightaway, in order to pay back this debt before it can get him in trouble. But on the way home on the yacht, Master seemed so anxious I didn't get a chance to raise the matter of what my percentage will be.

27 SEPTEMBER 1665

Master has been in a right nervous state about our business venture. I don't think he slept all night. He took me to Captain Cocke's house today, intent on telling the captain all the worries he had about "taking goods from the King without any Royal Permission." I've done my best to put him at ease, but all I got for thanks was Master cuffing me hard and asking me what I know.

"Nothing!" he answered for me.

As luck would have it the captain was out, so we went to see Mr Evelyn. This gentleman always soothes Master, because he never talks business. Today his chosen subject was on the Art of Painting. He said his wife was exceedingly good. Master said not the same about Mistress (nor did he mention my talent).

Then off to the Duke of Albemarle who made matters worse by saying that the Dutch are still out to make trouble, so the fleet should be back at sea.

"Lord Sandwich will be in disgrace at Court for sailing home with those prizes!"

Now Master fears the disgrace will be worse

if the Court hears about what he's taken. But the weekly Bill of Mortality is down for the first time in months; at least the plague seems to be easing.

1 OCTOBER 1665

Master went back on the yacht to see Lord Sandwich again, but this time he left me at home.

7 OCTOBER 1665

It has not been an easy week. Master is still apprehensive, and the city is crowded with seamen, many wrapped in dirty bandages, others sick, some starving to death. They're camping out in the streets and protesting noisily outside the Navy Office. They claim they haven't been paid; not for months. They've heard about the Dutch prizes, and how these have been filched away. They want their share of the profits. Windows are being smashed.

In the midst of all this two wagons turned up here from Rochester, loaded with our silks and spices. I was busy trying to unload them when the Customs men turned up too. I had to go and fetch Master. Angry words were exchanged. The officers only left when the goods were locked in our storehouse – "as property of His Majesty" – and the key had been handed over to the Constable. As soon as they'd gone the Constable said he'll do what he could to help get us out of trouble. Does this mean he wants a bribe?

I never found out. At this moment two men stumbled down the alleyway bearing a bloated plague corpse lolling on a stretcher. I ran for it, holding my nose. The plague hasn't got me in six long months; it's not going to catch me now!

11 OCTOBER 1665

Master is very busy, perhaps too busy to worry; he has been preparing more warships for sea, (succeeding with only seven, he says, out of twenty-two). But today we got a visit from one of the Commissioners for Prizes – a nasty, pompous man who told us all our goods will have to be confiscated. If so I will be in dead lumber, for Master will surely blame me for tempting him into this business. My star is not rising. Oh woe.

14 OCTOBER 1665

Some relief when Master returned tonight. He told
me that all his proposals for reform in the Navy
have been read out to the King, who gave them his
approval. In fact there will be a surveyor to
oversee all suppliers (and guess who that might
be?) If Master is in such favour at Court he should
see his way out of trouble over our other business.

"If you have His Majesty's ear, who can harm
you?" as Captain Cocke said. (I get the impression
that Master has plans to sell off his share to the
captain, who knows all the likely buyers.)

16 OCTOBER 1665

More good news: yesterday Parliament voted
another one-and-a-quarter million pounds, a
truly enormous sum. This should pay for the
costs of the war, so Master will have the funds to
supply all our ships with provisions – and pay
those angry seamen. Not that Master sees it this
way. He says the money can do little good before
the war is over – most likely won by the Dutch!
Our ships are not in good order, our sailors are
in revolt. "And then there's the plague," says
Master. "There is hardly a doctor left alive to
tend the sick!"

But at least a letter has come from Lord
Sandwich telling Master to have no fears about the
division of prize goods. The King himself has
agreed that nothing underhand was done, so that
is the end of the matter (except for my percentage).

15 November 1665

The plague is on the retreat, deaths from it down by 400, to under a thousand this week. Perhaps I will survive and become prosperous after all.

30 December 1665

The last day of the year, and what a year it has been. I now feel at home in London, but so far, what have I achieved?

I am now worth next to nothing (two shillings and four pence ha'penny) thanks to Colonel Blunt and the gross ingratitude of Master and Captain Cocke over my prize goods business. (When I brought up the subject Master professed amazement. He said, "The whole mad scheme was the crazy brain-child of that rogue of a captain." And if I had been behind it he would have sent me packing!) So much for my hopes for the future!

I've not had the chance to apply myself, except to running errands and dancing jigs with Mistress! This is surely all so unfair. My real talents have never been tested!

Pray God next year is better!

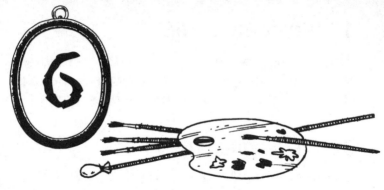

27 JANUARY 1666

The month has been windy and cold, the King
of Spain has died and the French have declared
war upon us, but nothing has happened to me –
except that last night I saw lights in the
Flatchetts' windows. The family must be back,
after long months in Suffolk, where they fled to
escape from the plague. However, I fear that
Mistress must have talked to Mrs Flatchett
about my lack of prospects. This afternoon
when we met in the street she hardly returned
my greeting, and Henrietta looked through me
as if I no longer existed. I sink even deeper
in woe.

1 FEBRUARY 1666

A new month, I must snap out of this gloom.
One needs to look on the bright side to find
one's way in this world. At least the plague has
died down.

3 FEBRUARY 1666

Mrs Flatchett visited (without her beautiful daughter). I overheard Mistress telling her that Mr Pepys is arranging to have her portrait painted by a certain Mr Hales. She thinks this a wasteful expense: "When he never looks at me anyway – and Master Scratch could paint me. He is quite a talented artist." (!)

4 FEBRUARY 1666

I've been wondering all day. Perhaps my mistake has been not trying to use my assets to their best advantage. Why waste any more of my time seeking a mind-numbing post on Master's Navy Board when I am a talented artist who should be following his genius? Who knows where this might lead! (Feel quite cheered up by the thought.)

15 FEBRUARY 1666

I went with Master to the artist's studio to see Mr Hales at work. He has started his portrait of Mistress. Mr Hales is a nervous man. I don't think he was too pleased to have Mrs Knipp turn up at the house. She is one of Mistress's friends, an actress at the King's playhouse. She suggested we sing a few songs. Mercer did her serious best and Master rose to the challenge. Of course, I have no voice to boast of: it cracks when it gets

too high. "Like a warbling frog," Master tells me.

So I watched Mr Hales with his brush. I told him that I'm an artist like him. I suggested we might help each other. This made him go "Humph!" Most conceited. However, I persisted, and Mistress put in a good word, so in the end he told me to bring along something I'd done, so that "he might be the judge".

23 FEBRUARY 1666

Lord Sandwich intends to leave for Spain today, so Master went to bid him farewell. Tonight we had a small party, with Mistress's friend, Mrs Knipp. Master had written a song for her. He called it *Beauty Retire*. She sang it for him several times. Master then persuaded her to act out one of the parts she has played in front of the King. She acted out lots of parts, and made them most melodramatic.

Afterwards Master commented, "What excellent company!" But Mistress seemed sulky.

25 FEBRUARY 1666

Lord Sandwich has been delayed, so Master and Mistress were summoned to go and stay at his house. They left me on my own to put a new plan into action, that is, to paint such a work of art to impress Mr Hales. So, setting out my paints on the table, I asked Susan to sit for me. I think I got a fair likeness. Tom's only comment was "Phwoorrrr!" I think this meant he liked it.

3 MARCH 1666

I complimented Mr Hales on his portrait. I pointed
out that the nose clearly posed him a challenge, as
he'd scrubbed it out several times, but I told him
the rest of the painting is perfectly good, in its way.

Yet when I showed him my portrait, the man
was no better than rude, saying the young lady's
bosom must have posed me a great challenge:
"An insurmountable challenge – it's totally out
of proportion!"

I asked him how he could judge, as he had not
seen the young lady's bosom! He said that he'd
rather like to.

15 March 1666

I went with Master when he collected the portrait. Mr Hales asked for £14 and Master said he deserved it! If Mr Hales could paint a bit faster he would soon be a very rich man. I swallowed my pride and asked him if he would give me some lessons. "What's in it for me?" he retorted. He is brusque as well as conceited.

17 March 1666

Back to Mr Hales. Master paid out the £14 (plus more for the cost of the frame!) and then it was his turn to sit, for he wants his portrait done too. Later I got the chance to talk with Mr Hales on the side. I admitted I wouldn't be able to pay for the painting lessons. "But I think I might find you more sitters," I said.

"How's that?" he asked.

"You must realise when I go about with my master I meet some very fine people. A word could be said in your favour."

I left him to think about this.

24 March 1666

Master came home from an audience with the Duke of York and told Mistress he had seen Lely (Who?) A great portrait painter at Court; he is

painting the Duchess of York. "Not half as good as Hales' portrait of you: all flattery, nothing of substance."

We could go far, me and Mr Hales, if only he was more generous. I could get him rich sitters, and while he is painting their portraits I could do their children and pets at a special discount price.

30 MARCH 1666

Master was in fine good form, having had a huge chest of coins delivered from Lombard Street where it had been for safe keeping from the time of the worst of the plague, earning a fair sum in interest.

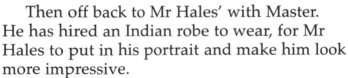

Then off back to Mr Hales' with Master. He has hired an Indian robe to wear, for Mr Hales to put in his portrait and make him look more impressive.

I soon got talking with Mr Hales about the painter Lely not being up to the mark. He said, "It's all right for Lely, he's got friends at Court."

I asked when my lessons could start.

He said, "You shall have your first lesson when you've brought along a new sitter."

6 APRIL 1666

It is announced that the Swedes have declared war against the Dutch, so they must now be our allies. I have been doing some sketching, of mythical temples with nymphs.

11 APRIL 1666

Master's portrait is finished, except for a final detail that Master has asked Mr Hales to add, showing him holding the musical score for the song he wrote, *Beauty Retire*. I'm surprised he doesn't want Mrs Knipp in the background too.

23 APRIL 1666

There are bonfires in the streets to mark the King's Coronation and St George's Day. I saw Mrs Flatchett with Henrietta (looking more lovely than ever). They were out for the first time in weeks, warming their hands from the flames. This gave me a useful idea – for killing two birds with one stone! When Mistress went up to greet them I hurried along behind and, when I got my chance, told them how fine the portraits are, that Mr Hales did for Master and Mistress. "Why not have your own portraits painted?"

Mrs Flatchett protested at the cost, so I said that Mr Flatchett could not make a better investment. "It would capture your beauty forever!"

I realised afterwards, I said this looking at her, instead of her beautiful daughter. She said I was very *gallant*.

28 MAY 1666

Another month has gone by but what a month it has been. My stratagem has succeeded! The two exquisite ladies have sat for Mr Hales and I have spent time at the studio, having my first two lessons. What's more I've had the chance to be near Henrietta, though so far I've not been able to talk with her by herself – her mother does most of the talking. As for Mr Hales, he told me in a sarcastic tone, that I'm better at temples than nymphs. Perhaps he is wasting my time. I might not find it so easy to bring him another client. Perhaps I should show my own work at Court. If I could get one commission from an earl or a duke, there would be no looking back! I might even talk to Lely.

I heard Henrietta tell Mr Hales if she was an artist she'd paint heroic scenes with sailors and fighting ships. Perhaps I should try one of these?

29 MAY 1666
RESTORATION DAY

The anniversary of the King's Restoration and also it's the King's birthday. God bless him, and

68

raise your goblets!

I confess I have drunk and I've drunk to the King, a little too often I think, for now that I am on my mattress the ceiling seems to sway and...

30 May 1666

Too ill to write.

1 June 1666
Fast Day

A Royal Proclamation states that this should be a Day of Fasting for all – no one is to eat any meat in order to gain divine favour. The Dutch are out in force. Very soon there might be a great battle and we need to have God on our side.

I filch a loaf from the kitchen to give me fuel to keep painting. Artists cannot live by rules like other, more ordinary men. My noble subject is *War at Sea*.

2 June 1666
Late at night

Frustrated, I have done no painting. Master woke me up with the news that the King has received a message from the Duke of Albemarle that our fleet is in sight of the Dutch, off the coast of northern France. Master was given the task of sending 200 soldiers to reinforce our sailors. We had to go to Blackwall Dock to see them on board transport ships. All their wives and children turned up, so there was much hugging and crying, though most of the soldiers were drunk. Some had to be laid on the decks. We could hear cannon fire up-river.

4 JUNE 1666

More gunfire heard down-river, though later we have a storm, so possibly it was only thunder. Master returned all gloomy. He had only been home a short while when there was a knock at the door. I opened it to find two men with their faces blackened by soot, claiming to be from the fleet. They were put ashore last night at Harwich and have ridden full tilt to give us news of the battle!

Master hurried them out of the house and down to Somerset Stairs where he hailed a rowing boat to take us up the river. And thus we made haste to the King, to tell him the happy news: that Prince Rupert's ships have re-joined with the Duke's to take on the Dutch fleet.

"So what is the outcome?" demanded the King.

The sailors looked worried. One spoke. "No, we was despatched, Your Great Majesty, Sire, to come 'ere and tell you the news... about the two fleets joining up, Sire; so we never witnessed no outcome."

I half-expected the King to order them both to be flogged, in fact, they would have deserved it! But putting his hand in his pocket, he bid them be on their way with a load of gold coins!

Is life fair? How could any man think so, when I have only two shillings and nine pence ha-penny left after more than a year's hard labour!

5 JUNE 1666

Everyone is still waiting, biting their fingernails, but I went to talk to Mr Hales; I have thought of a cunning ruse. I say I have been to Court and met an illustrious man. "A portrait could be in the offing," I say, "if you do me one small favour."

"What's that?" he asks, quick as a flash.

I suggest that he tells Mrs Flatchett he needs one extra session, but just with Henrietta.

"I don't, though. I've finished her face. It's the mother that's causing me problems."

"Henrietta's nose shouldn't look so turned up."

"It's not 'turned up'– it's pert!"

"All right," I conceded this point. "But please, just get her to come here, then you can go out for a walk and I can talk with her, Mr Hales, without her mother to hear us."

He says he will try to arrange it. I went home, feeling jaunty, and put the final touches to my masterpiece, *War at Sea*.

6 JUNE 1666
SUNDAY

Master went out seeking news. I escorted Mistress to church. Very dull service as usual until Master tiptoed in to join us during the sermon. He passed a hand-written message to me. It said: WE HAVE WON A GREAT VICTORY! MORE THAN HALF THE DUTCH FLEET DESTROYED! I passed the message to Mistress. It was handed from pew to pew. The parson was most irritated, until someone handed him the note, then he offered up grateful prayers.

7 JUNE 1666

I cannot believe this. Yesterday's news was all wrong. The latest is this, straight from Master at Court, that we did not win the battle. Instead, the Dutch have thrashed us!

13 JUNE 1666

Much better news! Mrs Flatchett has told Mistress how pleased she is with the portrait; and Mr Hales has asked for one more session to touch up her daughter a bit. Is this really how he put it? If so, the man is a rascal. But I'd better not risk having words until I have seen Henrietta!

14 JUNE 1666

It is arranged! Henrietta will be there tomorrow, at half-past four; so will I. I have now made a fateful decision. After I've shown her my painting, I shall declare my love!

I missed the meeting. Two-and-a-half months have gone by. I have been in a battle at sea.

28 AUGUST 1666

I am back in my cubby-hole, safely under the stairs in Mr Pepys's house; exhausted, having walked all the way from the docks at Chatham. Will Henrietta remember me? Has she noticed I've been away? Tom says she's been seen in a carriage "with a fine naval officer".

My confidence was further weakened when Mercer said, "What brings you here? We thought you'd gone home to Brampton."

At least Mistress showed some concern. She says I'm just skin and bone.

I'd better write down what has happened. Back on 15 July Master made the fateful decision to take me along to the funeral of a brave naval captain who had been killed in the battle, and I made the fateful decision to take a break from the service and slip out to a tavern nearby.

A couple of tankards later, mine host asked my line of trade, so like a fool I told him that I was a fashionable artist.

"And which of the famous beauties at Court have sat for you, eh?" (Nudge, wink.)

Not wanting to go into details I tried to change the subject. I said I could not be thinking of Art at this perilous time for our country. "The Dutch have defeated us, it's a disgrace. The Navy has let us down badly!"

"Oh, yes," says the tapster. "Hear that, lads?"

Only then did I turn and notice a whole gang of seamen between myself and the door.

"So what are you doing to help," one cried, "if you're such a naval expert?"

I spluttered that I could do nothing alone, but with their help, God save me. "If we could get hold of some fire-ships," I gasped, "and sail them among the Dutch ships, we could set them alight, that's the best way... to do the maximum damage with the least cost to ourselves!"

They grabbed me and dragged me outside. I feared I was going to be lynched, but at that moment a carriage passed by and one of these naval men called out to someone inside it.

"Sir William Coventry, Sir!"

Sir William stopped the carriage. The seamen gathered round.

Their leader, whose face was covered in scars, with half his left ear missing, claimed they had been at the funeral.

"It was for our own captain – the noble Sir Christopher Ming! All we have is our lives to offer, but give us a few old ships that we can fill with tar, Sir, and we will avenge his death by setting the Dutch ships ablaze!"

Sir William promised to tell the King about this daring proposal, but only as the carriage rolled off did I notice Master inside it. I shouted but it was too late. So I was forced to go back with my "friends" to drink some more toasts in the tavern.

I hoped to escape from these hotheads as soon as they'd drunk themselves stupid, but while they were all still singing (and making me sing along too) a gang of sailors barged into the tavern calling for "young volunteers". The landlord pointed at me.

"He's keen to fight for his Country!"

The drunkards hoisted me up. They clapped me hard on the back. Then the gang clapped me in irons.

The next few weeks were the worst of my life. I was taken to Bridewell Prison, shut up with three hundred others in a filthy and windowless cell, with hardly food or drink apart from disgusting slops. What a way to treat honest men, as if we were all common thieves! I put this

to our gaoler, and when he took no notice I
pointed out that I happened to know Mr Samuel
Pepys, Clerk to the Navy Board!

"Oh, do you?" he said. "Well, 'I happen to
know' the King, and the Pope. What about it?"
And after this he took pleasure in making jokes
about me in front of the other prisoners.

Then news came through that a great Dutch
fleet was mustering off Harwich. We were
ordered out of the prison. There were mothers
and wives in the street, all calling out to their
men on the most heartrending tones (though
nobody there for me – because no one knew of
my plight, not even dear Henrietta).

We were marched under guard to the river. A
vessel was waiting to take us down to Sheerness.

It was crowded, so we all had to stand. When we got there we were divided up into smaller groups and rowed out to different ships.

I was welcomed on board with ten others. The captain stood us in line and told us how lucky we were to have the chance to die for our King and Country.

He suddenly stared at me. "Good God, it's that fop of an artist!"

Only then did I recognise him. He had scars all over his face and half his ear was missing! Yes, he was the same naval man who had called to Sir William Coventry to get him the use of some fire-ships! I blathered, "Please Sir, could you save me!"

The captain, whose name it turned out was Holmes, clapped me hard on the back. "I could do with a hearty new servant. The last one was skewered by a Dutchman!"

So I was a servant again, of an even lowlier sort. I waited at the captain's table and kept his cabin scrubbed clean. In return I could sleep in his cabin instead of down on the gundeck, though sleeping wasn't that easy, swaying about in a hammock.

We sailed on 22 July, down the river and out to sea.

I'd never seen the sea before. It is bigger than I had expected, though there is nothing much to it but waves; so after a couple of days it was a welcome change to see the French coast on our right. "That's starboard to you!" snapped the captain when I pointed this out.

He said we had to stop the Dutch fleet from reaching the port of Calais where they wanted to pick up French soldiers, to transport them over the Channel and mount an invasion of England. To stop them we needed to fight them at sea!

On 25 July the fateful battle commenced.

I thought it was best to stay in the captain's cabin, so I could have his refreshments prepared for any short break from the fighting. But an officer thrust a musket and sword into my shaking hands and said I should die with the others. The captain was sailing our ship straight into the thick of the fray.

The crashing of gunfire was ghastly. I saw the *Resolution*, one of our finest ships, go up in a ball of flames, but Captain Holmes was unshaken. He managed to get our vessel side-on to a huge Dutch ship, and bellowed the order: "Engage! Every man for himself! Take no prisoners!"

Three Dutchmen jumped on our deck and came at me wielding their swords. I raised my musket in terror, but before I could open fire something heavy came down on my head. The next I knew I was flat on my back, and everything was white.

Was that it, was I really dead? Or safely back in my bed, after a dreadful nightmare? I was under some sort of a sheet but it was too heavy to shift.

It was only after the battle, when everything was quiet, that I found I could wriggle out. I had been buried under a sail. I stood up and saw the three Dutchmen all lying dead on the deck, squashed under a fallen mast. I turned round and saw Captain Holmes. His face had got three new scars, all bleeding profusely.

He grinned. "We've beaten them off. Well done, Scratch!" He was gloating, enjoying all this. But I didn't mind, if the Dutch fleet had fled. In fact I could see them retreating, up the coast back towards Holland. The trouble was that we now had to chase them.

Another two weeks with the fleet at sea, mighty seasick most of the time; but finally we found shelter at the mouth of a river just as the sun went down. I thought it was time for a break. But then Captain Holmes was calling: "I say, look at this!" He was pointing. I realised the estuary was crowded, the sky bristling full of Dutch masts. My heart sank. Would we have time to put out to sea again, before the enemy saw us? The captain grabbed hold of my elbow. He grinned at me fiercely: "Our chance, Scratch: we can make use of our fire-ships!"

SEA BATTLE – THE *RESOLUTION* BLOWS UP

Our "fire-ships" were several old tubs packed full of barrels of tar. They had to be towed inshore before they were set on fire, then left to drift on the rising tide further into the estuary. A few hours later the whole night sky was lit up with dozens of Dutch merchant ships blazing away like bonfires. I counted more than a hundred. It was a most frightful sight. But Captain Holmes wasn't satisfied. He was pacing about the deck. The fire seemed to make him go crazy. He ordered more boats to be lowered – to go on a "raiding party".

"We can set fire to the harbour as well, and then the town! Load your muskets!"

I had to go down to the cabin for mine. It took a long time to find it. By the time I got back on deck I seemed to have been left behind.

Mistress says I have been a great hero. Well, all I can say on the subject is this. That now I am safely back on dry land, in our great city of London, I hope that I never have to see anything else on fire, not ever again in my life.

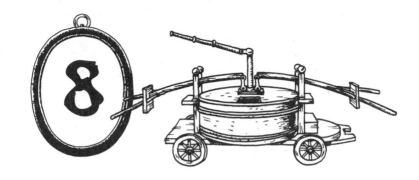

29 AUGUST 1666

Master and Mistress are off to a wedding but I am not invited. I hung about in the street for a while, hoping to see Henrietta, until Tom spied me and bellowed that I am "a sad looking dog".

A lot of work has been done while I've been away to refurbish Master's study. Master plans to hold a small party in a couple of days, to celebrate its completion. He has invited the Flatchetts, so Henrietta will come and then I will meet her again. I have decided to use my time preparing myself for this. I don't think I want to show her my painting of *War at Sea*; not now I've been in a battle. I would need to change certain details, and somehow I don't have the stomach for the task.

Putting more books on Master's shelves I came upon one of those volumes full of illustrations showing Italian villas. I realise I like drawing buildings. I might even try to design one. I feel this might be a better line for my artistic talents. Rather more practical too, if I could find a rich aristocrat who wanted a fine new house.

30 AUGUST 1666

Over the last two days I have been painting
again, producing a passable picture to show to
Henrietta – of a romantic palace surrounded by
woods and fields. This could be our home, I
might tell her, if ever I make my fortune. This
evening I walked along Seething Lane and came
face to face with the Flatchetts – mother and
daughter together. I blurted out a greeting. I
bowed. Then Henrietta screamed and ran away
down the street. Mrs Flatchett pulled a face. "We
thought you were dead," she said mildly.

1 SEPTEMBER 1666
NIGHT

I am unable to sleep. It is hot and my dreams are
crowded with battles and Henrietta. It is no good
dreaming about her. She exists and she lives so
close!

I went back to Master's study, intending to
look at his books, but picked up the spyglass he
uses to gaze at the heavens instead. I went onto
the roof where the party is going to be held. I
couldn't help angling the spyglass to have a
quick look in Henrietta's bedroom, and there she
was, in her white shift, brushing her long hair.

But as I adjusted the focus my hand slipped,
jogging the spyglass, and suddenly all I could
see was an ominous red glow from far away over
the rooftops. It filled my heart with dread – as if

I was back in my nightmare, with Captain Holmes and the Dutch snapping at my heels.

I rushed downstairs, and found Susan still at work in the kitchen preparing for Master's party. I told her my head was bursting with visions of buildings burning, whole streets of them, roaring flames! She said I was imagining things.

Distressed and feeling foolish, I crept back into my cubby-hole, only to be disturbed again, some time before the dawn, by Alice, the other maid, calling out to Master that there's a big fire in the town. Master went up on the roof (without having found his spyglass). He said, "It is near to Mark Lane, quite far away, so we should have nothing to fear."

4 September 1666

Master was wrong. I am writing this three days later, at Woolwich, with Mrs Pepys.

In the morning we heard the news that more than 300 houses had been burnt down in the night. The fire was still burning fiercely; it was spreading fast down Fish Street, nearly to London Bridge.

We hurried out after breakfast. We got as far as the Tower. The warden's son took us on its ramparts, from which we looked over the town. By now there were buildings burning not only on the north bank of the Thames but on London Bridge itself, and a few on the south side too, though it was hard to see clearly because there was so much smoke. It made me cough and my eyes sting.

THE GREAT FIRE
of LONDON

The boy said that the fire had first started in the house of a baker, Farrinor, in Pudding Lane. The Lord Mayor was told of it during the night, but wasn't worried. Apparently he went back to bed with the words: "Pish! A woman could piss it out!"

We took a boat from Tower Wharf, rowing westwards through London Bridge.

On the north bank we could see the fire spreading far up-river, fanned by a fierce dry wind. The spires of several churches were blazing like lighted torches and all along the waterfront were poor people loading boats with all their most precious possessions.

Master said we must go to the King directly. The watermen steered our boat to land at Whitehall Stairs.

At the Palace Master was welcomed and led away to the King's closet, while I was left in a corridor telling everyone else what we had seen of the fire. Then Master came out with orders to bring troops into the city and start demolishing buildings to stop the advancing fire. The Lord Mayor would have to be told.

Then who should we meet but Captain Cocke – who generously lent us his carriage to give us a lift to St Pauls. From here we hurried down Watling Street against a great flood of people all desperately fleeing the fire, some wheeling barrows and carts full of goods, with sick people carried on stretchers.

Before we could reach his residence we found the Lord Mayor in a panic, standing in Cannon

Street. He seemed not to understand what Master was trying to tell him. He shook his head, and flapped his hands: "The fire's too fierce. It carries hot sparks in the wind, they land in the thatch, Mr Pepys – the fire leaps over whole buildings! It's no use, I'm spent." There were tears in his eyes. "The city is doomed. It's all hopeless!"

Was he right? What more could we do? By now the fire was burning along the waterfront, setting light to the wharves and warehouses packed full of goods.

We went home, to find Master's guests had turned up. The Flatchetts and Henrietta were wide-eyed with fear and excitement. I blurted out all I had seen.

"Why, Master Scratch!" Mrs Flatchett exclaimed. "Mrs Pepys has just told us what a hero you've been, fighting at sea for our country; and now you've come home from the wars you go among burning buildings! I'd never have thought it of you!"

Henrietta gasped, "Oh, I would have." Her face was flushed, her eyes misty with what must have been admiration. She gazed up at me. "You're so modest."

I gazed back at her. I took her hand. My heart gave a lurch. "Henrietta–"

Then Master said, "Come along, Scratch. This is no time to hang about gabbling with women."

We took another boat to watch the fire from the water. The river was crowded with all kinds of craft, loaded down with people and goods, and boxes and bits and pieces bobbing about. We met with the King on his barge and went with him to Queenhithe where the Lord Mayor was waiting, a bit more composed this time. And we saw the first buildings being blown up with gunpowder to create gaps and stop the spread of the fire.

As evening finally fell we crossed by boat to the south bank and adjourned to a tavern at Southwark. The fire was a fierce blood red, flaring and churning with smoke, far away into the distance, as if the whole land was ablaze. But all I could think about was Henrietta's warm hand. My heart was aflame with great longing!

Back home we found Mistress frantically packing up goods, telling us that the fire was sure to reach Seething Lane and we must be ready to flee (the Flatchetts had fled already). So all of us set to work, carrying things out to the garden and digging deep holes in the ground in order to bury them safely – boxes of papers and silver, even barrels of wine and Master's rare Parmesan cheese.

At about four in the morning a cart turned up at the door to take his most prized possessions, including Mr Hales' portraits, to Mr William Ryder's house at Bethnal Green.

Next morning the work went on to transport

the goods we might need down to a landing stage and get them away to Woolwich.

We were out early the next morning, intent on getting away. The fire was now only two streets from our own front door. However everything was so chaotic that it was the afternoon before we pushed off from the wharf.

I escorted Mistress to Woolwich, where I am now in charge of getting the vessel unloaded, while Master goes back to the city – intent on saving more papers from the Navy Office.

7 SEPTEMBER 1666

I have returned to the city. What a bleak sight I beheld! Walking with Master down Fleet Street and through Ludgate, I saw the great walls of St Paul's Cathedral looming over the smouldering ruins of countless smaller buildings. It is a huge, gaunt empty shell. In many places we had to step smartly as the ground was still too hot to walk upon.

I reflected that this is a time when any normal man would be sure to have gloomy thoughts, but Master was not downcast. He clapped his hand on my back and told me, quietly but firmly: "The city will be rebuilt, Master Scratch, though there is much work to be done."

And suddenly I was inspired by having a grand idea – for why should it have to be re-built just like it was before? New buildings are going to be needed, so why not beautiful buildings like the ones that I have been sketching, in the Italian style?

This brought on another idea; for we will need gangs of builders, hundreds and hundreds of builders. I told this to Mr Pepys, that here is my chance come at last – to summon my brothers to London, so they can work under me, on projects I will obtain. And thus I will make my fortune and be able to ask Henrietta to be my darling wife; if Master will put in a few kind words with some of his powerful contacts?

Master gave me his slow, greasy smile, then shook his head with a chuckle, and looking out over the ruins he said, "Yes, I must help you, Scratch. You have been a good friend this last year. So here is what I will do. I'll use my influence to get you taken on by someone who knows about buildings. Mr Christopher Wren is the man. Train under him as a draughtsman and you might go far in this world. There is much to rebuild. It will take many years. There will be many plans, many projects. But right now we must be practical. Don't try to run before you can walk: we all have to start from SCRATCH!"

FACT FILE

LONDON

London had 300,000 inhabitants before the plague in 1665; it had rapidly grown to become the largest city in Europe. It was a centre for trade and manufacture and the biggest port in Britain with warehouses and wharves all along the river. But most buildings were small and cramped, with only St Paul's Cathedral, Westminster Abbey and the Banqueting Hall at Whitehall Palace rising above the skyline.

London Bridge was the only bridge spanning the River Thames. It had houses and shops built across it. The city itself was crowded, noisy and dirty from the smoke of coal fires. It had no proper sewers, only cesspits in the cellars or out in the backyard – often next to the well from which people drew their water.

SERVANTS

Most well-to-do households had several servants. It was also fairly common for any less fortunate relative to live in the house as a servant but eat with the family.

WAR WITH THE DUTCH

After being allies with the Dutch against the Spanish and French for many years, the Netherlands became England's rival for mastery of the sea and for the valuable trade with the East Indies. There were three Dutch Wars, from which the English finally emerged as victors. The war mentioned in this diary was the Second Dutch War which ended with the Treaty of Breda in 1667.

THE COURT

After years of poverty as an exile, Charles II wanted to enjoy himself. He lived extravagantly, rewarding his favourites and taking many mistresses (lovers). This didn't go down too well with the rest of the population, most of whom were poor or having to pay high taxes towards the cost of the war. In addition many people were intensely religious; the sort of lifestyle practised by the King was frowned upon.

THE ROYAL SOCIETY

This organisation was granted its charter by King Charles II in 1662. It was a centre for enquiry; to discover the laws that governed nature. Experiments were conducted on the transfusion of blood, the importance of oxygen and the laws of gravity, watched by members including Pepys, John Evelyn and Christopher Wren.

THE PLAGUE

This disease was caused by a bacterium, *Yersina pestis*, which lived in the bloodstream of infected black rats. It was passed from infected rats to humans by the bites of fleas. As people, rats and fleas all lived in close proximity to one another in 1665 the disease spread like wildfire.

Ten days after a bite from an infected flea the victim experienced terrible sweats, headaches and vomiting. Then the glands in their armpits and groin swelled up into enormous, agonisingly painful lumps called buboes. There was no known cure, and only a 30 per cent chance of survival. There had been four other outbreaks in the previous hundred years but the epidemic of 1665-6 was the worst, with 100,000 victims in London.

THE GREAT FIRE OF LONDON

This started in a bakery in Pudding Lane after a hot, dry summer. The fire spread fast through the narrow streets and wooden buildings, fanned by a fierce east wind. In four days and nights it burnt down more than 13,000 houses and 87 out of the city's 109 churches, including St Paul's Cathedral. The smoke could be seen from as far away as Oxford. Afterwards 200,000 Londoners had to camp out in the fields. It took several years to rebuild the city. With fire insurance not yet invented people had to pay all the costs of rebuilding themselves. The new houses were built of brick.

OTHER TITLES IN THIS SERIES

THE DIARY OF A YOUNG ROMAN SOLDIER
Marcus Gallo travels to Britain with his legion to help
pacify the wild Celtic tribes.

THE DIARY OF A YOUNG TUDOR LADY-IN WAITING
Young Rebecca Swann joins her aunt as a lady-in-
waiting to Queen Elizabeth the First.

THE DIARY OF A YOUNG NURSE IN WORLD WAR II
Jean Harris is hired to train as a nurse in a London
hospital just as World War II breaks out.

THE DIARY OF A YOUNG WEST INDIAN IMMIGRANT
It is 1961 and Gloria Charles travels from Dominica to
Britain to start a new life.

THE DIARY OF A 1960s TEENAGER
Teenager Jane Leachman is offered a job working in
swinging London's fashion industry.

THE DIARY OF A YOUNG ROMAN GIRL
It is AD74 and Secundia Fulvia Popillia is helping her
family prepare for her sister's wedding.

THE DIARY OF A YOUNG MEDIEVAL SQUIRE
It is 1332 and young William De Combe travels with
his uncle to a faraway jousting competition.

THE DIARY OF A WORLD WAR II PILOT
It is 1938 and young Johnny Hedley joins up to
become a pilot in Britain's Royal Air Force.